W9-BZK-343

TEEN TITANS GO!™

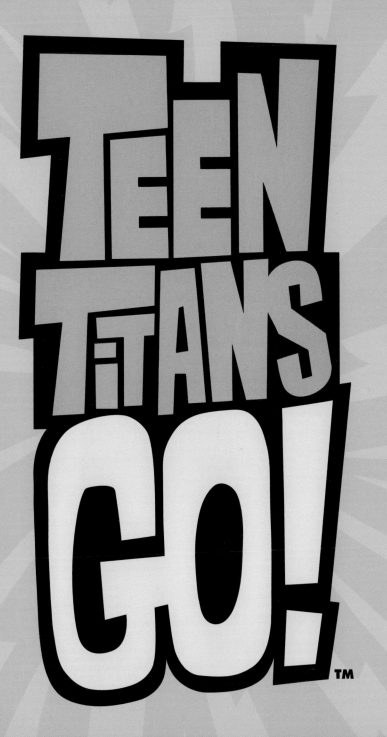

Copyright © 2016 DC Comics.
TEEN TITANS GO! and all related characters and elements
© & ™ DC Comics and Warner Bros. Entertainment Inc.
(s16)

All rights reserved. In accordance with the U.S. Copyright Act of 1976, the scanning, uploading, and electronic sharing of any part of this book without the permission of the publisher is unlawful piracy and theft of the author's intellectual property. If you would like to use material from the book (other than for review purposes), prior written permission must be obtained by contacting the publisher at permissions@hbgusa.com. Thank you for your support of the author's rights.

Little, Brown and Company

Hachette Book Group
1290 Avenue of the Americas, New York, NY 10104
Visit us at lb-kids.com

Little, Brown and Company is a division of Hachette Book Group, Inc.
The Little, Brown name and logo are trademarks of Hachette Book Group, Inc.

The publisher is not responsible for websites (or their content)
that are not owned by the publisher.

First Edition: September 2016

ISBN 978-0-316-35644-2

Library of Congress Control Number: 2016940588

10 9 8 7 6 5 4 3 2 1

CW

Printed in the United States of America

TEEN TITANS GO!

THE CRUEL GIGGLING GHOUL

Adapted by **Magnolia Belle**

Based on the episode **"The Cruel Giggling Ghoul"**

written by **Ben Gruber**

LITTLE, BROWN AND COMPANY
New York   Boston

Haverstraw King's Daughters
Public Library
10 West Ramapo Road
Garnerville, NY 10923

It is a dark and spooky night, and the Teen Titans are on their way to Wacka Doodles Amusement Park.

Robin is annoyed. "We wouldn't be so late if Cyborg and Beast Boy hadn't insisted on stopping for food every five minutes," he says.

"Hey, we were hungry, man." Cyborg says with a shrug.

Beast Boy notices Raven is wearing glasses.

"What's up with your peepers?" he asks her.

"I lost my contacts," Raven responds.

Beast Boy says, "Well, you look good with glasses, yo!"

After they've been in the van a long time, everybody gets restless.
Luckily Starfire thinks she sees the exit sign in the distance.
Bam! The sign hits her right in the face! But the good news is
they're only one mile away.

The Titans finally make it to the amusement park.

They all run for the entrance as Robin shouts, "Come on! Come on! We better hurry if we want to avoid all the lines!"

When they get there, the place is completely empty.

"Maybe we got here too early? There's nobody here!" Cyborg says.

The Teen Titans are weirded out at how empty and creepy the park is.

They start looking around for anybody that can explain why it's such a ghost town.

Lightning crashes and the Teen Titans gasp as the creepy amusement park manager appears out of nowhere.

He says, "They're gone. All of them. All the guests ran away the moment *it* showed up."

"*'It'*?" Cyborg gulps.

The manager peers around and answers, "The two-headed ghoul! It comes around on nights...just like tonight!"

Cyborg and Beast Boy start to run off. Beast Boy shouts, "I hate two-headed ghouls. We out, yo!"

Robin stops them. "Whoa, we are not leaving until we solve this mystery," he says.

"Do we have to? Ghouls are so scary!" Cyborg says, his voice quivering.

"This is even scarier than other ghouls!" the park manager says. "The only people left here are us, the park owner, and those two weirdos in the bumper cars." He points to the bumper cars, where Batman and Commissioner Gordon are giggling.

The manager continues, "I'd ask the owner for help, but he'll make millions from the insurance if this place goes under."

"Don't worry, creepy manager," Robin assures him. "The Titans are on the case."

Robin orders the Teen Titans to split up and look for clues.
Cyborg doesn't like the idea, but his mind changes when Beast Boy
points out a delicious aroma coming from the Snack Shack.

"Uh, yeah, let's split up! Beast Boy and I will
investigate the Snack Shack!" Cyborg shouts.
"Let's check the owner's office for clues,"
Robin commands the rest of the gang.

Beast Boy and Cyborg look for clues inside giant sandwiches.

"*Mm-mmm*, my favorite! A triple-decker sardine, jelly, and tomato sandwich!" Cyborg cries.

Beast Boy says, "Not bad, but check out my quadruple triple-decker veggie sammie!"

Cyborg hears an eerie giggle coming from inside the Snack Shack. "Ahhh! It's the ghoul!" Cyborg screams. "Let's get out of here!"

The giggling two-headed ghoul bursts out of the Snack Shack and chases after Beast Boy and Cyborg.

He chases them into the fun house.
And around the Ferris wheel.
Soon, Beast Boy and Cyborg realize
they'll have better luck tricking the ghoul.
A distraction helps them get away.

Haverstraw King's
Daughters Public Library

In the owner's office, the other Teen Titans rifle through documents. Raven finds a clue.

The pages show that attendance at the park has gone up since bumper cars were added.

"The owner can't be happy about that if he wants this place to lose money," Robin says.

The park owner bursts in and scares the Titans. "What are you doing in my office?" he shouts.

Robin responds, "We're trying to get to the bottom of this ghoul mystery."

The owner growls, "All I see are three groovy teens pawing through my stuff. Get out!"

Outside the owner's office, Starfire finds a secret passage. It leads to access tunnels under the entire park.

They follow a tunnel to a row of lockers holding mascot costumes. There's an empty locker with strange footprints in front of it.

Raven investigates, saying, "Two sets of boot prints. I know the ghoul has two heads—but not four feet! Something is not right here."

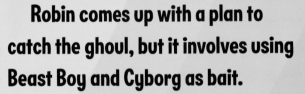

Robin comes up with a plan to catch the ghoul, but it involves using Beast Boy and Cyborg as bait.

Beast Boy doesn't like that idea. "No way, yo!" he shouts.

"Would you do it for a burrito?" Raven asks.

"For sure!" Cyborg answers. "And I'd do it for a burger!"

Beast Boy and Cyborg wait outside the bumper cars with their burrito and burger while the other Teen Titans hide nearby.

Cyborg talks loudly, "Oh no! I *cannot* believe how lost we are." Then he whispers to Beast Boy, "No ghoul is dumb enough to fall for this."

Suddenly, the two-headed ghoul shows up. Robin jumps out and shouts, "Gotcha!"

The two-headed ghoul hops into a bumper car and tries to get away.

The Teen Titans chase after him!

Cyborg and Beast Boy throw their burger and burrito in both of the ghoul's ugly faces, and he crashes.

"Time to unmask this ghoul," Robin declares as he pulls off their phony faces.

Everyone gasps and says, "Batman and Commissioner Gordon?!"

"But why would they do all this?" Cyborg asks.

"Simple. Their favorite ride, the bumper cars, was becoming too popular," Robin explains. "So Batman and Commissioner Gordon dressed up like the two-headed ghoul to scare everyone away."

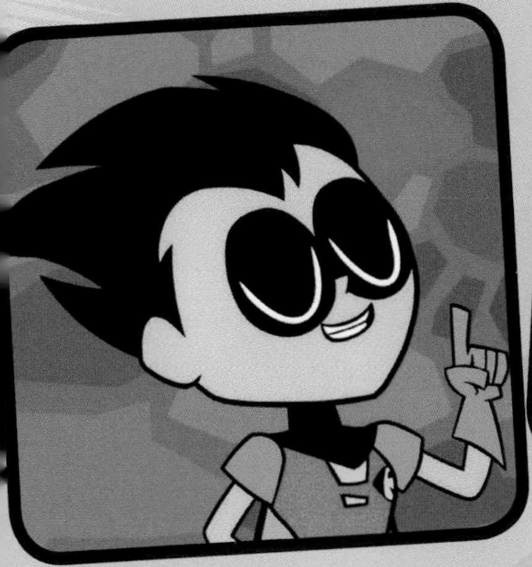

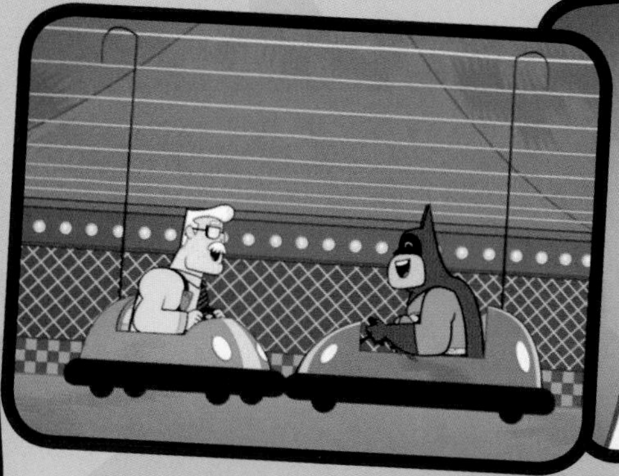

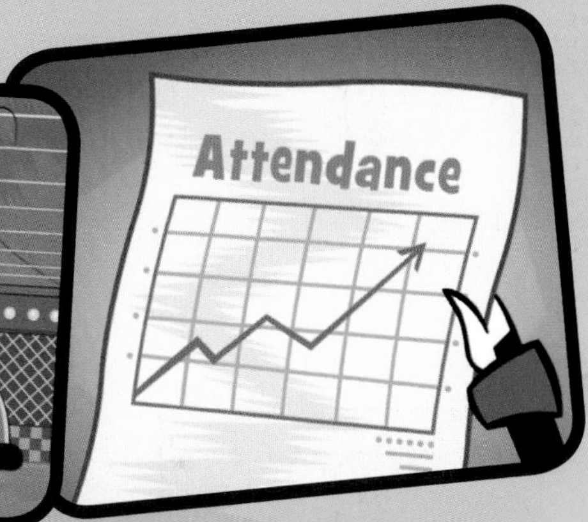
Attendance

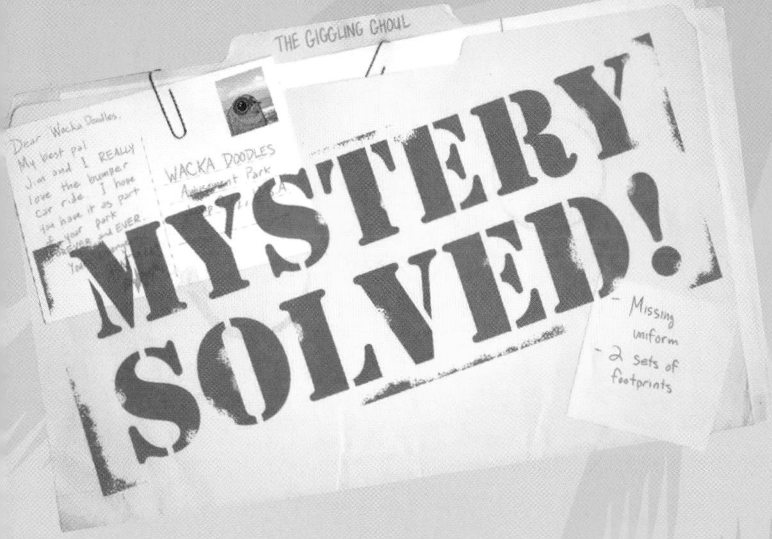
THE GIGGLING GHOUL
Dear Wacka Doodles,
My best pal Jim and I REALLY love the bumper car ride. I hope you have it as part
WACKA DOODLES
Amusement Park
MYSTERY SOLVED!
- Missing uniform
- 2 sets of footprints

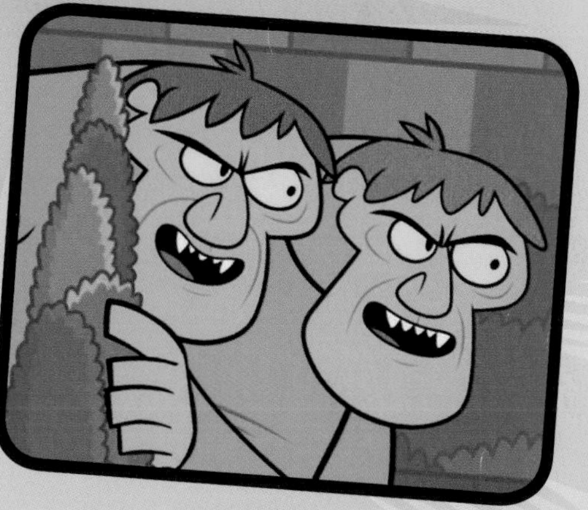

Raven laughs. "Of course. With no other guests, they'd never have to wait in line."

"And they would have gotten away with it, too, if it weren't for us meddling kids," Beast Boy says. And everybody laughs. Even Batman.